Phoenix Young Readers Library

The Adventures of Thiga

Phoenix Young Readers Library

1. Lots of Wonders — Sam Mbure
2. The Sun and the Wind — Anne Matindi
3. Tha Pet Snake — Dickson Mukunyi
4. The Greedy Host — J.K. Njoroge
5. The Speck of Gold — Cynthia Hunter
6. The Peacock and the Snake — Elijah K. Soi
7. Cock and Lion — Kalondu Kyendo
8. Beautiful Nyakio — Frederick Ndungu
9. Children of the Forest — Joel Makumi
10. Mzee Nyachote — Roeland Japuonjo
11. The Fly Whisk — Stephen Gichuru
12. The Talking Devil — Leo Odera Omolo
13. The Feather in the Lake — Joel Makumi
14. Give the Devil his Due — W.K. Boruett
15. Inspector Rajabu Investigates — F. Kawegere
16. The Powerful Magician — Daniel Irungu
17. End of the Beginning — Joel Makumi
18. Onyango's Triumph — Leo Odera Omolo
19. Tales of Wamugumo — Peter N. Kuguru
20. The Girl Who Couldn't Keep a Secret — Clare Omanga
21. Wake Up and Open Your Eyes — Edward Muhire
22. The Proud Ostrich — J.K. Njoroge
23. Njogu the Prophet — Jamlick Mutua
24. Travels of a Raindrop — David Ngosos
25. The Adventures of Thiga — C.M. Mureithi
26. Pamela the Probation Officer — Cynthia Hunter
27. Anna the Air Hostess — Cynthia Hunter
28. The Circle of Revenge — David Mwaurah
29. The Town Tricksters — David Mwaurah
30. Truphena Student Nurse — Cynthia Hunter
31. Truphena City Nurse — Cynthia Hunter
32. The River Without Frogs — Writers' Committee
33. The Great Siege of Fort Jesus — Valerie Cuthbert
34. Captured by Raiders — Benjamin S. Wegesa
35. Njaga the Town Monkey — Joel Makumi

and more………many more

The Adventures of Thiga

C.M. Mureithi
Illustrations: Chris Ochieng
Cover: Julius Maina

PHOENIX PUBLISHERS, NAIROBI

Phoenix Publishers,
First published In 1971
This edition published in 1989 by
Phoenix Publishers Ltd.,
Mellow Heights, Ngara Road,
P.O Box 30474-00100,
Nairobi.

© C.M Mureithi, 1971,1988
© Illustrations: Phoenix Publishers Ltd.

ISBN 9966 47 075 1

Reprinted in 1991, 1993, 1994, 1996,1998,1999, 2001, 2002, 2003, 2004, 2008, 2010, 2013, 2016, 2019

Printed by
Modern Lithographic (K) Limited,
P.0 52810-00200,
Nairobi, Kenya.

Contents

1. The immovable rock 1
2. What Thiga found under the rock 12
3. The mountain giant 16
4. Another escape 24
5. The palace of torture 29
6. The gaily-dressed murderer 40
7. The three-eyed giant 47
8. Thiga reaches his father's kingdom 53

1

The immovable rock

A long time ago there was a man and his wife who lived in a small village. The man was very greedy and kept on telling his wife she never gave him enough food. The wife did not know how to satisfy him as the more she gave him, the more he grumbled.

The time came for her to give birth to a baby boy. They called him Thiga. He was a lovely child, strong and healthy. He grew up to fear nothing, except the quarrels between his parents.

Thiga's mother worked and worked in order to grow as much food as she could. She bought the biggest pot in the market so that she could cook a large amount for every meal. But although her husband ate all the food except a small portion she set aside for herself and her son, he was still not satisfied. She tried to cultivate more land to grow more crops, but her lazy husband would not help her with the digging or weeding.

After some years, Thiga's mother grew thinner and thinner through overwork. Every morning she went to the shamba and stayed there until half an hour before sunset. Then she hurried home, carrying a heavy load of firewood on her back, a water pot on her head, and the baby, Thiga, also tied on her back on top of the firewood.

As soon as she got home, she started to prepare an enormous meal for her greedy husband, who spent his days sitting in the sun or visiting his friends.

When Thiga was about two years old, she knew that her husband would never change, so she decided to take her son and run away. All she wanted was to live in peace and care for her child.

Early one morning, while her husband was still sleeping, she packed a few belongings into a large basket. She also took some food and two gourds of water. Then she tied her small son to her back and started on her journey. She was determined to go as far away as possible, so that her husband would never find them.

She made her way through thick forests, up hills and down valleys, across plains and through deserted bush country. She was afraid she might meet wild animals, ghosts or giants. All the folktales her grandmother had told her about these creatures kept coming into her mind.

However, although she travelled a long way, she did

not come across any of the dangers which she had feared. She could not carry food for more than a few days, so she had to look for nuts and fruits for Thiga and herself. She only found just enough to keep them alive, so that they were very thin and weak when they arrived in their new country. Thiga's mother chose a place where she hoped her greedy husband would not be able to find them. There she built a small shelter for herself and her child and started to cultivate the soil.

She found life very hard for the first few months, as she had to beg for food from the surrounding villages to keep themselves alive until her own crops ripened. Luckily she had brought good seed from her homeland and the new soil was fertile, so after the first season all was well.

Thiga was too young to know the hardships his mother was suffering, but he was a good boy, and as he grew older he helped her more and more.

He did not remember his father and he never asked about him.

The years passed. Thiga and his mother built a new house and cultivated more land. They made many friends and lived comfortably in their new home. Thiga grew up to be a tall, handsome young man and he had many girlfriends. He was good at sports, especially wrestling and fighting, both with his hands and with spears and clubs.

He was stronger than most of the young men of his age-group and he nearly always won a fight. The other young men both respected him and feared him.

The country where Thiga and his mother had settled was very flat, but there was a small hill near the village. The hill was surrounded by thick bushes, and near the top there was a huge tree. Nobody knew how long the tree had been there, but they said it had been growing for hundreds of years. There was an enormous stone beside the tree. It had appeared during a night of heavy rain soon after Thiga and his mother had arrived in the district. Some people said it must have fallen from the skies; others said the gods had put it there; some said it had been rolled up to the top by giants. But nobody really knew. How the enormous stone got there was always a mystery.

Thiga often walked up to the top of the hill to look at the surrounding countryside. He could see for many miles and it was very beautiful. One fine morning, Thiga's mother walked to the bottom of the hill with him.

"You are brave and strong, my son," she said. "Climb up to that huge stone by the large tree and roll the stone down the hillside. Then bring me what lies underneath."

"I'll do as you say, Mother," said Thiga. "But what is there under the stone?" He could not understand why his mother had not told him what to look for.

"Just bring me whatever you find underneath it," replied his mother. "That's all I want."

Thiga was still puzzled, but he did not argue with his mother. He walked quickly up the hill with long strides. He was very curious to know what was under the large stone. When he reached the tree, he rested for a few minutes and looked at the stone. It appeared to be larger than ever and had sunk deep into the ground.

"I'll never be able to roll that down the hill," he said to himself. "Nobody could do that alone, however strong he was."

He walked towards the stone and stood looking at it. He tried to think how he could possibly move it at all. He walked all round it. It had become so smooth and slippery with the rain and wind beating against it that there was no grip for his hands. He sat down and tried to think what to do.

"My mother has told me I must roll this stone down the hill," he said aloud. "Somehow I must do what she says."

He stood up and stretched his whole body. Then he put his hands on one side of the stone and pushed with all his strength. The stone would not move an inch. He pushed again and again. He pushed until he was so tired that he had to sit down and rest, but still nothing happened. The rock remained in the same place.

"Shall I give up?" he thought. His head hurt and his back hurt, and there was a burning pain in his hands. He was shivering with the effort he had made, and at the same time he was sweating all over.

After a while he knew he must try and try again and again until he was able to roll the stone down the hill. He could not go back and tell his mother he had failed. He got up and tried again and again, but it was no good. Slowly he walked down the hill to the place where his mother was waiting. He stood beside her and turned his head away. He was ashamed to look into her eyes.

"Mother, I've tried and tried with all my might, but I couldn't move the stone even an inch," he said. "I really don't think a dozen men could move that great rock from its bed."

Thiga's mother felt sorry for her son.

"My son," she said. "Even if you fail, you mustn't give up. You might have to try a second, a third, or even a fourth time, but in the end you will succeed. We'll go home now, and in one year's time you can try again."

Thiga felt encouraged by his mother's words, although he was too upset to ask her again what was hidden under the rock. He lay awake that night wondering what to do. He was quite sure that no normal man could move the rock, so he decided he must gain a great deal more strength.

"I'll start first thing tomorrow morning," he said. "I'll challenge every young man in my age-group to all kinds of games. I mustn't ever be the loser. I must win every wrestling and boxing match, every spear-throwing competition, and every running and obstacle race."

The months went by and the young men got tired of competing against Thiga. They greatly respected him, but as he always won, they said there was no point in fighting against him. They agreed to make him their champion and could not give him any higher honour than that.

"You're stronger than any of us," they all said.

But that was not enough for Thiga. Arming himself with a sword, a spear and a club, he went into the forest to fight with the wild animals. He killed leopards, lions and rhinos with his weapons. Then he went unarmed into the forest and still he fought and killed many wild animals. Sometimes he returned home badly wounded and his mother tried to stop him going into the forest alone. But when he told her he was gaining strength in order to roll the huge rock down the hill, she told him to do what he thought best.

Exactly a year from the day his mother had taken him to the bottom of the hill and told him what she wanted him to do, Thiga went back and climbed up to the top and rested by the tree. After a while, he tried and tried to move the huge rock from its bed, but again he did not succeed. After many hours, he sadly returned to the house where his mother was waiting.

From the look on his face, she knew at once that her son had failed once again. But she told him not to give up hope.

"I'm not giving up," he agreed. "If I have to try a third, fourth, fifth or even a tenth time, one day I shall do as you ask. I'll push the stone down the hill and bring you whatever lies underneath."

His mother tried not to show her disappointment. She knew that her son would succeed one day, but she would not tell him what she wanted from under the stone. "The more curious he is, the more he will want to do as I ask," she said to herself.

Thiga wished his mother would tell him what lay under the rock.

"If only I knew what I was looking for, I'd try even harder," he said as he tried to persuade her to tell him the secret.

"You must gain in strength, my son," she said. "You must go on trying until you can do what I ask."

Year after year, Thiga did everything he could to make himself strong, but each time he tried to push the rock from its bed, he failed. He became more and more miserable and at last his mother began to get impatient.

It was five years since his mother had first told him her wish.

"My son, I've waited long enough," she said in a firm voice. "I'm worried now that you're a weakling. Today you must prove I'm wrong. We'll go together to the bottom of the hill. Then you'll climb to the top and push the rock down. I'll wait and wait until you succeed. This time you will not fail. This time you must not return until your task is completed."

"Very well, Mother," replied Thiga. "I'll go with you today. I'll try and try and I'll go on trying until I succeed."

He spoke with more courage than he felt as he went towards the hill with his mother. He left her at the bottom of the path, and without a word he climbed to the top. Up, up, up he went, and this time, instead of resting by the tree, he went straight to the rock and stood leaning against it.

"Today will be my real test of strength," he thought. "I'll die on this spot rather than disappoint my mother again."

He stood up beside the rock with his feet wide apart. He thrust his arms forwards and opened his hands. He pushed against the rock with all his strength. It did not move. He tried again and again and again. He tried until his hands were sore and every part of his body ached with strain. Still he pushed the rock, and when he felt he had no more strength even to stand, he pushed yet again. The rock remained firmly embedded in the soil.

He sat down and cursed the rock. Then he stood up once more, and pushed with the strength of a madman. But still without success. Tears ran down his cheeks. Tears of anger and pain. Tears that mixed with the sweat on his face and dropped onto the unmoving rock. He fell to the ground in a deep sleep, and as he slept he dreamt that he had rolled the rock down the hill. He awoke filled with joy and started to run down the hill back to his mother. When he was half-way down, he realised he was carrying nothing in his hands. He ran back to pick up whatever was buried under the rock, but of course the rock was still there.

"It was only a dream!" he cried and he felt he would die of disappointment.

"Now or never!" he said aloud.

He rushed at the rock, pressing his lips and teeth closely together. He took a deep breath and pushed with all the strength he had gained in those five long years. The rock moved a little. He let go and leapt into the air with joy. The rock rolled back again and settled in its bed of earth.

"Why did I get so excited? Oh why did I let go?"

He cursed himself. He cursed the rock. He cursed the earth that held the rock in its firm grip. He rested for a few moments to gather up his strength once more.

"At least it moves," he thought. "This time I'll go on pushing, even if I die in the attempt."

He thrust his hands and feet at the rock with all his might. He was just about to stop and rest once more when he felt a slight movement. His strength had almost left him, but he closed his eyes and made one more effort. Suddenly, he fell forward on his face. There was a noise of thunder, as the huge rock started to roll faster and faster down the hill.

2

What Thiga found under the rock

At first Thiga could not believe his eyes as the enormous stone gathered speed and rolled over and over towards the bottom of the hill. His cries of joy rang through the air as he ran towards his mother. In his excitement, he had forgotten to pick up the things beneath the rock; in fact, he had not even looked to see what was there!

Half-way down he remembered and ran back and looked into the hole that the rock had left in the earth. There was a sword and a pair of sandals, nothing more. He picked them up and ran back to his mother, shouting happily all the way.

"I knew I could do it! I knew I could do it!" he shouted.

"I knew you could do it!" came his mother's answering cry, as he ran towards her, waving the sword and the sandals above his head.

The joyful moments did not last long. As soon as Thiga reached his mother, she hurried away from him and covered her face with her hands. He saw she was weeping. He stood beside her, wondering what to say. Then she uncovered her eyes and asked him to follow her to the top of the hill. She was still weeping and Thiga could not understand why she was not overjoyed with his success. He began to feel annoyed that she had not even given one word of praise. Why should she cry so bitterly when he had worked so hard for five long years to gain the strength to do as she had asked? Her tears were not tears of joy.

They walked to the top of the hill in silence and stood beside the hole left by the huge rock. The mother did not even look at the place where the stone had lain for so long, but gazed far into the distance. For a long moment, mother and son stood in silence. Then Thiga's mother spoke.

"Look at the land below us as far as you can see. It's very beautiful. There are pastures and forests, lakes and rivers. The country is very rich. It is a land which produces good crops and fine, fat cattle. What would you do if you were the king of that country?" she asked.

Thiga was very surprised at her question, but he answered quietly.

"I would rule the land wisely, justly and boldly," he said. "I would encourage the people to work hard with their hands and to cultivate the land and look after their cattle. I would try to make all the people happy, and after my death everyone would call me 'the Great Farmer King.'"

"Then carry the sword and sandals which you're holding, and take them to the king of that country," said his mother. "Tell the king that it was you who rolled away the rock from the hill, and show him the sword and sandals. Then ask him who hid them under the rock."

Thiga thought for a moment that his mother must have gone mad. He could not understand why she was giving him these orders without any explanation. However, he had always obeyed her without question, so he decided he must do as she told him. He turned to go, but when he looked back, he saw his mother was weeping again.

"Why do you send me away, Mother, now I have done what you asked?" said Thiga.

In reply, she put her hand over Thiga's mouth.

"My son, you must do as I say, but perhaps I should tell you that this is the last time you will see me. — But go now," she said quickly. "Any more delay will break my heart."

Thiga felt heavy with grief. How could his mother torture him so? She had always been so kind and thoughtful towards him, but now she was sending him off to a strange land without giving him any reason. He wanted to know more about the king of this land, and why he should be able to tell him who had hidden the sword and the sandals.

He stood for a moment not knowing what to do. Then his mother moved quickly towards him and embraced him fondly.

"I know you won't fail me," she said. Those were the last words he ever heard her speak. She let him go and walked quickly away, while Thiga sat down and tried to sort out his thoughts.

3

The mountain giant

Thiga sat for a long time wondering whether he should follow his mother home. But custom was stronger than his wishes. He knew he had to obey his mother even if it was a torture to him.

"She must know what she's doing. She must have a good reason for sending me away," he said to himself. This thought made him feel better, and his worry now was how to get to the king's palace. He felt frightened and wondered if the king would be pleased to see him or not. Then he remembered that when he was a small boy his mother had told him she had heard that his father had changed his ways after she had left him, and had become a great king somewhere. She had said very little else about him, and he had asked no questions.

Thiga knew he must set off on his journey, but he decided to take a long time about it. He thought he should try to do something important first, so that he would win the king's favour. Even if this unknown king turned out to be his father, he would have other sons. He would most likely value them far more than Thiga, whom he had not seen since he was a baby. Thiga would have to think of a plan to impress the king. He thought and thought, but nothing came into his mind. He could think of no great deeds that had not already been done before.

It was getting late and Thiga began to feel hungry. He went into the nearby bush to find some fruit and nuts. Darkness had fallen by the time he had gathered enough food for his evening meal. He made a fire at the edge of the bush and prepared a bed of leaves. He was afraid of falling asleep in case the fire went out and wild animals came and carried him off. But when he had eaten his food, his eyes closed and he found it was impossible to stay awake. He slept soundly until late the following morning.

For several days Thiga lived by the edge of the bush. He killed rabbits and antelopes for his food and cooked the meat over a wood fire. All the time he kept thinking of ways to impress the strange king, and of the brave deeds he could perform. One evening, when he was half asleep, thoughts of giants came into his mind.

"That's the idea," he cried. "I'll travel on and find a giant that has been troubling the king's people. I'll track him to his castle and kill him. The news of my bravery will reach the king before I arrive, and when he knows I'm nearby, he'll want to meet me. As soon as we meet, I'll give him the sword and sandals. Surely then he'll accept me into his household."

The next day Thiga started out on his journey. He felt more at ease than he had done since the day he had rolled the great rock down the hill.

The trees were close together and the undergrowth was very thick. It was difficult for Thiga to see where he was going. He travelled on for several weeks through forest and clearing and across open grassland. He did not meet any wild animals or any giants, although he was always looking out for them.

At last he came to the place called The Mountain of the Spider. It was called this because a great giant lived there. He killed people and slowly drank the blood from their veins, like spiders do to the flies they catch in their cobwebs. Of course, as Thiga was a stranger, he did not know about this, but when he was near the mountain, a sudden fear seized him. He held his sword and spear ready to use quickly in case of need, and walked on looking to right and left as he went. He had not gone much farther when he saw the giant of The Mountain of the Spider lying full length on a rocky ledge. Thiga gazed at the giant, but kept on walking. He saw he was wearing a beautiful robe made of leopard skins, and he had an elephant's skull on his head which was decorated with ostrich feathers.

The giant lay still watching Thiga.

"That looks like a strong man," he said to himself. "I'll suck his blood and his strength will flow into me."

"Ha, ha, ha, ha, ha!" the giant gave a terrifying laugh, but lay still on the ledge.

Thiga walked on. He was not easily frightened.

Then the giant pointed a huge finger at Thiga and called to him to come near him. Thiga went on walking.

"Who are you?" roared the giant. "How dare you come into my land and disobey my orders!"

When Thiga did not reply, the giant shouted even louder. "I'll have no mercy on you," he went on. "I'll suck all the blood from your veins until you have no strength left. Then you'll slowly die."

Thiga went on walking, but clutched his sword and spear more tightly. He wanted the giant to challenge him to a fight. "Who are you?" he asked the giant. "How can you want to be so cruel as to kill a stranger who has done you no harm?"

"You're a very daring young man," the giant roared, and the whole forest rang with the sound of his voice. "Come here at once, so I can suck your blood. Don't try to run away, you won't get very far. Ha, ha, ha, ha, ha!"

Thiga was now very annoyed that the giant expected him to give in without even a fight.

"Maybe you've sucked blood from other travellers, but you won't be able to do so from me," said Thiga firmly. Courage flowed into his veins, and he was quite prepared to attack the giant.

The giant sat up and lifted a huge club that lay near his feet. "My father gave me this club," he said, lifting it higher into the air. "I use it to beat rude strangers like you into powder."

"This sword was given to me by my mother to defend myself against cruel beasts such as you," shouted Thiga bravely in reply.

"Bring that sword here, or I'll strike you dead," roared the giant in a wild fury.

Thiga knew the giant wanted to kill him, but he bravely rushed towards him, waving the sword. He ran to one side to avoid the giant's leg as he thrust it towards him in a mighty kick. As the giant drew back his foot for another blow, Thiga struck out with his sword and cut him below the ankle. The giant groaned and lay down again. Blood poured from the wound and he cried out in pain and anger. Thiga hit him again and again until the great roars quietened and finally stopped. The Giant of the Mountain of the Spider would never again suck the blood of strangers who passed through his country. Thiga had killed him.

Thiga walked slowly away from the mountain and after a few days he came to a green valley. There he found a spring of pure, cold water and he knelt down to drink. At once he felt refreshed, but he knew he needed food and rest before he continued his journey. He lay beside the spring for a while and looked around him. Not far away he saw a herd of cattle and knew there were ordinary people living there. It was not a land of giants.

His spirits rose as he got up and walked towards the herdsman who was guarding the cattle. He greeted him and then told him how he had killed the Giant of the Mountain of the Spider. The herdsman called the people of the surrounding district together and Thiga repeated his story. At first, they did not believe he had killed such a terrible monster, and they sent some brave warriors to go and see for themselves. When they returned, carrying a piece of the giant's hair and some of the ostrich feathers that decorated his head-dress, they all praised Thiga. They slaughtered a bull and arranged a feast in his honour. They begged him to stay with them. They said they would feed him and give him some cattle if he would protect them from their enemies.

"I thank you for the wonderful way you've treated me. I've very much enjoyed my visit to you," Thiga told the friendly people. "But I must continue my journey because of a promise I made to my mother."

The people respected his decision. They gave him a farewell feast and packed up enough food to last him for the next few days. He thanked them again for their kindness and went on his way.

4

Another escape

Thiga said goodbye to the herdsmen of the green valley and travelled on through a highly populated area. As there were so many people, he had no fear of giants or wild animals attacking him in the daytime, and by night he was given shelter in one of the huts. Then the land became wilder, and Thiga had to pass through many forests, each one thicker than the last.

One day, he walked along a narrow path where the trees were so close together that he could hardly pass by without touching them. It was almost dark, because the branches met overhead and stopped the sun coming through. Thiga sensed danger. For the first time since his journey had begun, he felt really frightened. Nothing happened until he arrived at the edge of the forest. There in a large clearing he saw a huge giant near a pile of sisal ropes. He was holding an enormous club, as if he was ready to strike anyone who came near him. Hundreds of human bodies and skeletons lay scattered around the place where he was sitting. Some were hanging on trees and others were lying on the ground. It was a horrible sight, and Thiga was more frightened than ever. He knew that this giant must need to eat a large number of people to keep himself alive.

Then he realized that the giant was staring at him. Thiga stared back. The giant said nothing, but pointed to one of the skeletons with his club. Thiga knew what the sign meant, and the two stared at each other for a long time. At last the giant broke the silence.

"Many days have passed since a human body was added to my store. You have come here without an invitation, so you will become as one of those." He pointed to one of the skeletons hanging on a tree and smiled a cruel smile.

Thiga bravely walked towards the giant, holding his sword tightly. He watched carefully for any movement the giant might make. This was the first time the giant had ever seen a man who dared to walk towards him without trembling. Every other person had always run away as fast as he could, only to be caught by the giant after a few yards. The giant was very angry when he saw Thiga walking towards him instead of running away.

The next moment Thiga found himself held high up in the air in the giant's hand. He hit the giant with his sword

just as he was going to throw him on the ground. There was a small wound in the giant's throat which bled slightly, otherwise he was unharmed. Thiga's great strength seemed like that of a child when compared with that of the giant.

Once again the giant lifted Thiga up and tried to throw him to the ground, but once again Thiga stopped himself falling. This time he twisted his legs round the giant's hand so he could not shake him off. All the time Thiga made fierce, sword thrusts at the giant until he was bleeding from so many places that he fell down in a faint. As he fell, Thiga dropped from his hand and ran off as fast as he could. The giant recovered enough to sit up, and when he saw his victim running away, he hurled his club after him. The club hit Thiga in the middle of his back and made him fall over. The pain was too great for him to stand up, so he crawled deep into the bush and hid. He hoped the giant would not be able to find him because he was badly hurt and had to rest for several days.

Luckily for Thiga, his back was not broken, but he was badly bruised and suffering from shock. He made his way slowly through the bush, and after some weeks he reached a friendly village. The village doctor treated his back and a family, whose son had been killed by the giant, gave Thiga a bed and provided him with food until he was well enough to continue his journey.

For many months he travelled on without anything happening to him. But as every day took him farther and farther away from his mother, he thought more and more about her. He still hoped he would see her again one day, but he kept remembering her words: "This is the last time you'll see me," and "I know you won't fail me." He wondered if she was still alive, and if he would perhaps see her when he had completed his mission.

"I must hurry on and find the king," he said to himself. "Then I can go back home quickly and perhaps my mother will still be alive."

5

The palace of torture

Another few months passed, and Thiga travelled on peacefully. People were helpful and kind when he told them the purpose of his journey was to fulfil his mother's last wish. They gave him food and shelter and told him where he must go to find the king of the beautiful land.

One morning, Thiga came to a market which was just across the border of the land of a cruel king. It was market-day, and the place was full of people buying and selling and exchanging goods.

Thiga went up to a man who was looking after a stall and asked him the way to the kingdom he was searching for. Instead of answering, the man gave him a scared look and ran away. Thiga looked after him, wondering why he behaved like that. Then he saw the man returning with a group of others. They looked fierce and frightening as they surrounded Thiga. Although he was a good fighter, he knew he could not possibly win single-handed against so many. But the men did not try to attack the stranger.

"Young man, why do you want to go to your death?" asked the man he had first spoken to.

Thiga was surprised at this question.

"What have I done to make you think I'm going to be killed?" he asked in his turn.

"Don't you know that the king of this land does not allow any stranger inside his kingdom?" replied the man. He was amazed that Thiga did not seem to know about the cruel king.

"If the king knew you were here, he would send fierce soldiers to capture you and take you to his palace. Then he would take great pleasure in seeing you put to death in a most unpleasant way," the man explained. "You'd better leave here at once, before he knows about you and sends his men to arrest you."

Thiga was glad that the men themselves felt no ill will towards him. They only wanted to help him and were worried about his safety.

"It's kind of you all to worry about my safety," said Thiga. "But I must fulfil my mission, because it is what my mother has asked me to do. It may be her dying wish."

The men again tried to persuade Thiga to go back, but the young man told them of the dangers he had already passed through on his travels.

"Several times I nearly died," he said. "But I have travelled for so long and have come so far, that I can't turn back now because of the cruel king. I'll go to the palace and ask him to let me pass peacefully through his land. I'm not the kind of person to run away from danger."

One after another the men begged Thiga to return. They said he was going to certain death if he let the king know he was a stranger in the land. However, when they found that Thiga was determined to go to the palace, they gave him directions to get there quickly.

"Why does such a fine young man put his life in danger when there's no need?" one person said to another, as they stood in the marketplace and watched Thiga go on his way with firm strides.

They thought he must be crazy, or perhaps he did not understand the danger he was in. Some of them ran after him and once again tried to persuade him to change his mind. Thiga stopped and told them how he had already escaped from two giants and how he had killed one of them.

"The cruel king can't be as bad as a giant," he said. He thanked them again for their help and once more set off towards the palace. The people were afraid that they would be seen talking to the stranger and that the king would get to know and punish them. So they hurried back to the marketplace, feeling annoyed with Thiga for not taking their advice. But they were also sorry for him because they thought he would surely die.

It took Thiga three more days to reach the palace of the cruel king, which was right in the middle of his land.

Fierce soldiers were guarding the gate and asked him who he was and what business he had with the king.

"Tell the king I'm a stranger in the land," said Thiga boldly.

The soldiers were amazed at such daring words.

"We shall tell the king," one of them answered.

"Ask him if he will fight the stranger tonight!" shouted Thiga, as the soldier went through the palace gates.

The soldier could hardly believe his ears. He stopped and looked at Thiga for several minutes.

Then he told the others to guard him well and went off to see the king.

When the king heard about the daring stranger, he was also amazed. He told the soldier to bring Thiga to him at once.

A group of soldiers surrounded Thiga and marched him into the king's dining-room where he was sitting at the table having his evening meal. He looked at Thiga and laughed. He thought he must be a crazy young man to come into the palace of torture and death uninvited.

"Leave him with me," he ordered the soldiers, and laughed again.

He thought he would easily kill Thiga as he had done all the other strangers who had come to his land. But when he saw the young man standing up straight in front of him, not looking at all frightened, he could not help admiring him.

"This young man has courage," he thought. "I'm lonely," he said aloud. "Would you like to join me in the evening meal?"

Thiga thought this was a hopeful sign. He was also hungry, so he gratefully accepted the king's offer. The king pointed to a chair at the opposite end of a long table, and told Thiga to sit down.

There was a great deal of food laid out, including a bull which had been roasted whole.

"You may start eating," said the king. He tore the roasted bull apart with his hands and ate quickly, taking enormous mouthfuls.

Thiga was hungry and ate almost enough for three men, but he was shocked to find the heavily laden table completely empty of food at the end of the meal. The king sat contentedly, chewing the large bone of one of the legs of the bull.

"Is he a man or a giant?" wondered Thiga, and fear began to creep into his bones.

When the king was satisfied, he got up and told Thiga to follow him. They went into another room and a servant brought two calabashes of beer. He put one in front of the king and the other in front of Thiga. Then he left them alone together. The king drank in enormous gulps, but Thiga sipped his beer slowly. He thought that the king was now going to show his cruelty by first getting him drunk in order to kill him easily.

The king finished his calabash of beer and called for some more. The servant also put a second calabash in front of Thiga and took the first one away. Thiga hoped the king would think he had finished all the beer. On the other hand, if the king was as cruel as the people in the market had said, why had he given him food and drink? Perhaps the people had not told him the truth. Perhaps they had heard of Thiga's bravery and were jealous of him, and thought the king would reward him for his courage, or make him one of his advisors. All these thoughts went through Thiga's mind as he sat watching the king as he drank slowly from the second calabash of beer.

When the king had finished drinking, he looked up at Thiga.

"I'm known to be the strongest man that ever lived," he said at last. "Yet you've challenged me to a fight. Very well, tonight we'll have a wrestling match, and tomorrow we'll have a fight."

He got up and Thiga followed him to the hall where the palace games were played. Without a word of warning, the king rushed at Thiga and the contest began. They were both very strong, but the king was obviously the stronger of the two. Thiga was glad that he had not drunk too much beer. He tried all the tricks he knew and there was a great struggle as each tried to knock the other down. The king became angry. He had never fought with anybody like Thiga before. He expected to shake him like a rat and knock him senseless at the first blow. When he realised how strong Thiga was, he caught hold of his throat and tried to strangle him, Thiga quickly managed to free himself and the struggle continued.

Suddenly Thiga slipped and before he recovered his balance, the king knocked him down and lay on top of him. The struggle continued on the ground; but Thiga made a great effort and somehow managed to free himself yet again from the king's grasp and stood up. He was sweating, panting and very tired, but determined to continue the fight. However, the king also stood up and said in a firm voice that the day's wrestling was over.

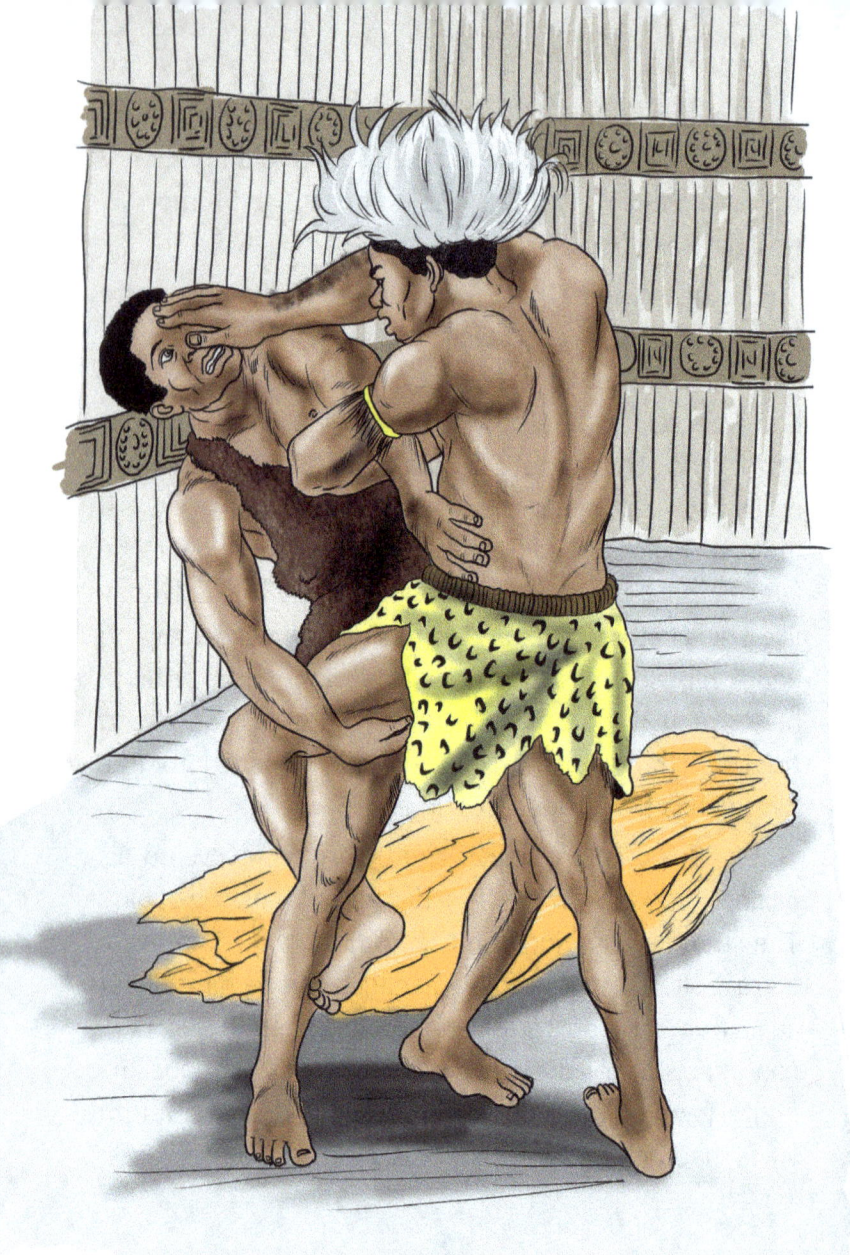

Thiga wanted to carry on. He felt sure he would now beat the king, but there was nothing more he could do. The king called a servant and told him to take Thiga to a small room and lock him in for the night. When he left him, he told Thiga to be prepared to fight again early the following morning. This time it was not to be a wrestling match, but a fight with swords.

That night, neither the king nor Thiga slept well. Each was thinking about the fight and trying to remember every trick that would help him to become the winner.

Early in the morning, the king sent for two swords. He ordered one to be given to Thiga.

"Unlock his door and take him some food," he told one of the servants. "Give him this sword and tell him to come to the hall in an hour's time."

Thiga did as he was told, and again as soon as he entered the long room, the king rushed at him almost before he was ready. The duel started at once. It was fierce and exciting. They each tried out all the tricks they knew. They were both determined to win, but neither thought the fight would be so hard. They knew it was a fight to the death, but they were both so clever that they both managed to defend themselves or dodge away from the worst blows. Sweat dropped from their bodies and their breath came in quick gasps. Sometimes one of them nearly fell, but managed to recover before the other rushed upon him. It seemed that the fight would never end.

Thiga was almost at the end of his strength. He made one last effort to pierce the king's heart with his sword. He missed, but gave him a mighty blow. The king fell down and at once Thiga gave another thrust, but the king kicked him away. This made him drop his sword and before he could bend to pick it up, the king was on his feet again. Thiga was quite helpless without his sword, but rushed at the king with the strength of a desperate man, making him drop his sword also. They were now locked together in a final, unarmed combat.

Suddenly Thiga managed to push himself free for an instant. He picked up his sword and gave a deadly thrust at the king, who rolled on his side and crumpled up in a dying heap.

For a moment Thiga could not believe that the king was defeated and dead. Gradually, he realised how lucky he was, and that it might have been himself lying lifeless in the dust, and not the cruel king.

News of the death of the brutal king spread like fire amongst the people all over the land. No one could believe that he had been killed by a man stronger than himself. They thought that no one could be stronger than their king. However, it did not take them long to realize that the reign of terror was over, and they all rejoiced in Thiga's deed of bravery in ridding them of their cruel king. Now their friends from foreign lands could visit them without fear of being tortured and killed. They sent a group of elders to ask Thiga if he would be their next ruler. He was very tempted by their offer, but he refused. He told them that he had a mission to travel to many countries and kill robbers, giants, and even kings, who troubled innocent people. He also told them he had to travel on until he found the king of the beautiful land, and so fulfil his mother's command.

"My mother told me to present the king with this sword and these sandals which I have carried throughout all my adventures," he said.

The people respected Thiga and sent him on his way with their blessing.

6

The gaily-dressed murderer

Thiga said farewell to the people he had freed from the cruel king. They elected another leader and were happy in their choice.

So Thiga travelled on to find the king of the beautiful land, the land he had seen with his mother from the hill: the hill where he had at last managed to dislodge the huge stone and roll it down: the hill where he had found the sword and sandals which he still carried.

In a few days he came to another hill, surrounded by thick forest. He felt tired and he walked slowly. However, his legs were long, so he covered the ground faster than most people. In front of him he saw a gaily-dressed man, who was walking even more slowly. As he came towards him, the man greeted him politely and asked where he was going. Thiga told him, and the man seemed to be very interested. He noticed that Thiga was very tired.

"Why don't you spend the night in my house?" he asked. "Then tomorrow you'll be able to continue your journey feeling fresh and well."

Thiga gratefully accepted the invitation. He was indeed tired. He was also hungry, and the idea of an evening meal and sleeping in a house pleased him very much. They walked on together, talking in a friendly way, until a man and a donkey appeared some distance behind them. The 'clip-clop' of the donkey's hooves could easily be heard on the hard soil. The gaily-dressed man turned and saw him. Then he asked Thiga to wait while he ran back to talk to the man. He told Thiga the man with the donkey was a great friend whom he had not seen for a long time.

The gaily-dressed man hurried back while Thiga walked slowly onwards, waiting for him to catch up. A few yards ahead, Thiga saw an old man who was struggling to carry a large load of firewood.

"Young man, help me to lift this load on to my back," called the old man.

Thiga helped him tie the load across his back, and while he waited the old man asked him who he was and where he was going.

"I'm a stranger here," said Thiga. "I'm looking for the king of the beautiful country. I've been travelling for many months, and I can't be far away now."

"You've helped me," said the old man. "Now I'll help you in return. I'm old and feeble, and my life has nearly come to an end. But you are young and have many years before you. Listen to me and I can save your life."

"Save my life, from what?" exclaimed Thiga in surprise. "My life's been saved many times, but at present I'm in no danger."

"You think you're in no danger," replied the old man sadly. "You're heading towards the den of death, murder and misery. That gaily-dressed man who spoke to you just now is my master. He's a cunning, deceitful person; he's a murderer and a robber. Whenever he sees a stranger like you, he invites him to stay the night in his house. That stranger is never seen again."

"Tell me more about your master," said Thiga, wondering whether or not the old man was telling the truth.

"He has a golden bed," went on the old man. "He offers this bed to any stranger who accepts his invitation to spend the night in his house. In the middle of the night, he ties the man to the bed. If his legs are too short he pulls and pulls until the man reaches from one end of the bed to the other. If they're too long, he cuts them off with a sharp sword. Either way means death to the victim. This is how this wicked man gets his pleasure, and afterwards he takes all the possessions from the murdered man. That is how he has become rich over the years. He is quite mad."

"So that's why the man asked me to spend the night in his house, is it?" said Thiga, half to himself. "Yet he seemed so kind and understanding. He seemed to be really sorry to see me looking so tired. He must be mad if the old man is telling the truth. What a terrible way to gain your pleasure, torturing people like that."

"If this is true, then why hasn't your master killed you?" asked Thiga. "Why should he spare you if he takes so much pleasure in killing everyone else?"

He suddenly wondered if the old man was deceiving him and if he was really a giant trying to trap him.

"My son, I was just about your age when I was enticed into my master's house. I was also very rich. This wicked man would have killed me in the same way as the others, but when I lay down on the bed, he found that I fitted exactly! There was not an inch to spare top or bottom, so he could neither pull my legs nor cut them off. He was so surprised that anyone should be the exact size of the golden bed, that he spared my life. But he took away all my riches and I have had to work for him ever since. He's never married, so he makes me do a woman's work. I gather firewood, carry water, and cook and clean the house."

Thiga felt sorry for the old man, but he could not help being amused to think of the murderer's surprise when he saw his victim exactly fitting the bed.

"Hurry away before my wicked master catches up with you," said the old man. "Don't be led to the house of murder."

Thiga still wondered if the old man was playing a trick on him and if he was really telling the truth.

"Old man," he said. "How is it that you're so old and your master is so young? Yet you say he captured you when you were as young as I am?"

"All I can tell you is that my master never seems to get older, while I seem to age two years at a time."

Thiga thanked the old man, who went on his way carrying his load. Not long afterwards the gaily-dressed man caught up with Thiga, who had decided not to run away, but to risk going to the man's house. The man with the donkey also joined them and the three walked along together.

The two friends talked about different people in the district, and Thiga decided to ask if there was a wicked man who lived nearby who cut off the legs of strangers and also robbed them. As he spoke, Thiga looked up at the face of the man who had invited him to stay. The man's face turned gray and he answered in a halting voice.

"I've heard such stories of a man like that who lives near one of the hills of this region, but I've never known anybody who's met him."

From the tone of his voice and the look on his face, Thiga now knew that this gaily-dressed man must indeed be the robber and the murderer which the old man had told him about. He knew he must be careful, but he went on talking.

"Surely if you've lived in this district all your life, you would have known if such a man existed? You would have found out about him and tried to destroy him!"

The man now began to suspect that Thiga knew who he was, and he did not answer his last remark. The thing that Thiga did not know was that the man with the donkey was also a stranger, and that the gaily-dressed man was planning to kill them both. They walked on in silence until Thiga noticed the man was trying to unsheath his sword without anyone noticing. He rushed at his would-be murderer and threw him to the ground. The man with the donkey fled and left the other two fighting for their lives.

"Tell me the truth," said Thiga. He had overpowered his enemy for the moment. "Are you the person who murders strangers in this horrible way?"

The man did not answer. Thiga shook the man furiously and then threw him away from him. Then they both faced each other again, ready with their swords.

Thiga waited calmly, but the other man rushed towards him like a madman, Thiga jumped to one side and hit the man's elbow, making his sword fall out of his hand. It was the murderer's turn to plead for mercy for the first time in his life.

"Lead me to your house," demanded Thiga.

The gay clothes of the murderer were now in rags and he walked with slow steps towards his house. The old man who had been his slave for so many years, helped to tie the murderer to his own bed. Thiga then told him to go and fetch the village elders. He killed the man who had been a terror to the area for so many years, and helped the elders divide his riches amongst the people.

7

The three-eyed giant

The elders of the district where Thiga had killed the murderer begged him to stay. But Thiga gave his usual reply that he must continue his mission. By now he had been through so many kinds of dangers that he had no more fear of the unknown. He journeyed on for several weeks until one cold, misty morning he came to a valley which was dotted with boulders. By the side of one of these huge rocks, he saw an old man trying to warm himself by a dying fire.

When Thiga came up to him, he saw that the man was very old indeed and had long, white hair over his forehead which reached down to his eyes.

"Can I share your fire, old man?" asked Thiga. "It's certainly very cold this morning."

The old man welcomed him, Thiga sat down by the side of the fire and the two started talking. A strong wind began blowing and lifted the hair off the old man's forehead. He tried to turn away, but he was too late. Thiga had already seen a third eye, like a piece of burning charcoal, above the old man's nose. Thiga realized he was once more facing a fierce giant.

After a few minutes, he thanked the old man for his company and said he had warmed himself enough and must now hurry on to his destination. The old man looked steadily into the fire and did not reply. Thiga got up and walked away as quickly as he could, but within five minutes the old man, now in the form of a giant, hurried past him. He stopped at a small hill not far ahead. There was nothing Thiga could do but to walk towards him.

This giant was smaller than those that Thiga had met so far. As he reached the hill where the giant was sitting, he saw an elephant's bone lying close to his feet.

"He must kill people with that bone," thought Thiga. He walked on, but the giant called to him.

When Thiga took no notice, he called him a rat and a pig and other bad names.

Thiga walked on, pretending not to hear. The giant then roared at him and at the same time shot out a jet of burning water which fell onto Thiga. It came from the giant's third eye, which was now glowing more brightly than before.

What a fiercesome weapon! As the water fell on his skin, Thiga felt a terrible itching all over his body. He started to scratch himself, but this made the burning even more painful. For the first time since he had begun his journey, Thiga felt he was defeated. He could fight and beat anybody, man or giant, using bows, arrows and spears, but what weapon could he use to defeat a person who could spurt out this terrible, burning water at him?

He continued scratching his body, but it only became worse and started to swell up. "What can I do?" he kept thinking, although he could hardly bear the pain. "If this giant does this again, it will be the end of me."

Quickly he broke a huge branch off a tree and threw it at the giant's third eye. Unfortunately for Thiga, it hit the giant's nose instead, and this made more water rush out of the terrible, burning eye towards Thiga. Thiga dodged to one side and rushed forward to miss the terrible stream. He looked up and saw the giant pick up the huge elephant's bone and prepare to hit him. Whenever Thiga jumped to one side, the giant quickly turned his head to aim more water at him. Thiga noticed a large club lying on the ground. He picked it up and ran towards the giant and threw it at the horrible eye with all his might. The giant gave a thunderous scream and the elephant's bone fell from his hand. The giant's eye closed.

Now both Thiga and the giant were mad with pain, but each was still determined to kill the other. The giant got up and took a step towards Thiga. Thiga ran away and the giant ran after him. Neither could move very fast as they were in such pain, but several times the giant nearly caught up with Thiga because his stride was so long. Thiga thought quickly. The only way to save his life was to trap the giant. He turned to face him. The giant thought he had given up the struggle and lifted his great foot in the air to kick him. At that moment, Thiga struck out with his sword and made a deep cut in the giant's foot. The giant fell to the ground, but as he did so, he sent another stream of water towards Thiga. They were now both rolling about with pain, but Thiga managed to strike a deep blow at the giant's head before becoming unconscious.

It was some hours before Thiga came to his senses. He felt sick and dizzy and his body was swollen from head to foot. He managed to raise himself on his elbow and saw the giant lying dead a few yards away. Thiga lay where he had fallen, growing weak with hunger and thirst. Slowly his body became less painful and the swelling went down. At last he managed to crawl along on his hands and knees until he came to a village. He stopped at the first house and just managed to ask for food and shelter before he collapsed once more.

Luckily for Thiga, he had chosen the house belonging to a kindly old couple who took him in and treated him as their son. They cared for him for many weeks until he was fit enough to continue his journey.

8

Thiga reaches his father's kingdom

Once again Thiga continued his journey in search of the beautiful kingdom, but this time it was only a few days before he realized he had reached his destination. For some reason he felt sadness in his heart instead of joy. He wondered what was in store for him.

As he looked round, he saw that it was indeed a very beautiful land. In the far distance he could just make out the outline of the hill where he had said goodbye to his mother, so long ago. He looked down at the sword and sandals he still carried, and wondered how he had managed to save them through all his adventures. Now he must find the king and give them to him. Then he would learn the meaning of his journey.

"What shall I do?" he cried. "What shall I do?" he wondered. Would he never see her again, as she had said?

He longed to talk to her and to tell her he had fulfilled his mission. He missed her more now than he had done since his journey began. He wanted her advice as to what to do next.

"What shall I do?" he cried. "What shall I do?"

He had never before wanted anybody's help or advice. He had always been glad to make his own decisions. He thought he would go and seek the help of a witch doctor. He had seen the signs of such a man outside a cave about half a mile back.

The witch doctor was surprised to see a stranger. He was even more surprised when he learnt about Thiga's adventures and how far he had come.

"I have spilt much blood on my journey," said Thiga. "I fear that the future may be bad for me because of this."

The witch doctor looked at Thiga and asked if he had killed anyone without good cause.

"I've only killed giants and evil men," said Thiga. "And I can also truly say I've only killed them in self-defence."

The witch doctor picked up a small gourd and shook it several times. Then he opened it and poured some seeds on the ground and examined the position in which they had fallen.

"I see a good future for you," said the witchdoctor, staring first at the seeds and then at Thiga. "But there is still a hard task awaiting you before you can settle down to a peaceful life. All this time your mother has been thinking of you and sending you her blessing. It is due to her that you've passed safely through so many dangers, and you're still alive."

Thiga thanked the witch doctor for what he had told him. He now felt much more cheerful. He asked him to direct him to the king's palace, and once more went on his way in good spirits.

When he arrived at the palace, a large feast was being held for one of the king's sons. A soldier stopped Thiga at the palace gates and asked him what he wanted.

"I want to see the king," replied Thiga.

"What does a man in shabby clothes like yours want to see the king for?" asked the soldier.

"I have been sent on a mission to his kingdom, and I have travelled many, many miles," replied Thiga. "Please tell the king I want to see him."

The soldier first went and reported Thiga's request to one of the princes.

"What kind of mission brings you here?" the prince asked when he saw Thiga standing patiently outside the gates.

"I'm afraid I can tell no one but the king himself," replied Thiga.

The prince looked at him scornfully and was going to turn him away, but something in Thiga's manner stopped him.

"Take him to the servant's quarters and give him some food and let him wash. Then bring him back to me in my room," ordered the prince.

Thiga was allowed through the palace gates and was led along many passages before he came to the kitchens. He was taken to a small room where he was given a large bowl of delicious stew. Thiga was very hungry, and he had not enjoyed such good food since the last meal his mother had cooked for him so long ago.

When he had finished eating, a servant came to fetch him and took him to a large room where all the king's sons were assembled.

"They certainly don't look very friendly," thought Thiga.

The eldest prince spoke.

"No one is allowed into the king's presence until we've heard his request first. The king has given us orders to deal with everyone who wants to see him. You may only see him if we can't come to a decision ourselves."

This was a problem to Thiga. He wanted to tell the king about his journey and how he had killed the giants. He wanted to tell him about his adventures and all the dangers he had overcome. He hoped to make a good impression, but somehow he did not think the king's sons would take much notice of his stories. He did not want to hand over the sword and sandals to them or tell them about his mother and the true purpose of his mission. He therefore refused to tell princes why he had come, and kept on saying he must see the king as soon as possible.

Then the youngest son spoke up. "I've heard about his adventures," he said. "He's a murderer. Let's chase him away."

The eldest son disagreed.

"If he's just an adventurer and a murderer, why should he walk into the king's palace where he knows he might be thrown into prison or killed?"

The princes started quarrelling amongst themselves, and in the end they decided that Thiga had better see the king.

"Our father, the king, will have to decide what to do with this man," said the eldest son. "I'll go and tell him he's here."

It was not long before Thiga was escorted to the king's own room. There was no need for Thiga to talk about the trials of his journey. The king had already heard of his brave deeds, and he greatly admired Thiga.

"This evening, I will call my sons and all my advisors and leaders into the great hall and you shall tell them about your adventures in your own words," said the king.

He then called a servant and told him to take Thiga to one of the guest rooms in the palace so he could rest. He also ordered fine new clothes to be made ready for him by the evening.

For reasons they could not even explain to themselves, the princes were jealous of Thiga. However, they could not help being interested in hearing about his adventures, and the districts he had passed through on his way to their land.

Evening came and a servant was sent to fetch Thiga. He quickly dressed himself in fine new robes of beautiful skins, and followed the servant to the great hall. There appeared to be hundreds of people waiting for him. The servant led him to a raised platform beside the king and his sons, and told him to begin his tale. Thiga started from the time he left his own country, but he did not mention his mother, nor did he say anything about the sword or the sandals, which he had hidden beneath his cloak.

After about an hour, Thiga had only told half his story. The king decided to give him a rest, and have food and drink served to the guests. The queen, who had stayed in another room while Thiga was speaking, now appeared in front of him for the first time. She was very beautiful.

She poured some drink into a special cup and handed it to Thiga.

"I have heard you are a great hero," she said. "This drink will refresh you and also make sure the wounds you received on your journey are completely healed."

Thiga took the cup and lifted it up.

"I drink to the king and queen of this land," he said in a loud voice.

But instead of raising the glass to his own lips, he handed it back to the queen.

"It is the custom in my land for our host or hostess to have the honour to take a sip first from the drink she gives to her guest."

The queen took the glass and stood watching Thiga with a horrified look on her face. She gazed at the king and then back to Thiga. What he had suspected was true. She had put poison in Thiga's drink, and the king knew about it too.

There was silence in the hall as the queen dropped the cup, spilling the contents all over the floor. Then she walked quickly out of the hall, followed by the princes.

Everyone started talking at once and the king and Thiga angrily faced each other. Then Thiga pulled out the sword and sandals and held them high above his head.

"See, the big rock has been rolled away. My mother made me try every year until I could move it. Here are the sword and sandals which were hidden underneath. She told me to bring them to you, although she did not tell me who had hidden them or why I should go to find your beautiful land."

"My son! My son!" cried the king in a loud deep voice.

Everyone in the hall heard his words and stopped talking. They looked towards the king and saw him embracing Thiga.

"This is my long lost son," he told the people.

They all shouted and stamped for joy. The noise reached the princes, who came back to see what was happening.

"This is my eldest son, your brother, who has been lost for so many years," he told them.

The princes were angry. They thought that Thiga had tricked the king, who would now leave him the biggest share of his kingdom. They drew their swords and rushed at Thiga. But Thiga wanted no more bloodshed. He stood unarmed before them, and asked them to welcome him as a brother.

They refused to listen to him, but moved towards him. The king called to his sons to leave Thiga alone, but by this time they were wild with fury. Thiga thought his last moment had come, but he snatched up the sword he had given his father a few moments before, and tried to defend himself.

He struck out at one of the princes, who immediately fell to the ground. The others fled. The fallen prince stood up slowly. To his shame, he had fallen to the ground with fear, and not because Thiga had harmed him.

The king called all his sons back and made them shake hands with Thiga and settle their quarrel.

"I was a lazy, good-for-nothing man," he told them all. "I nearly killed my dear first wife because I made her work so hard. In the end she ran away, taking our only child with her. She reached the land where my father before me had lived and where he had buried this sword and these sandals under a great rock. She sent me a message telling me not to follow her, but to send her my news from time to time. She told me that when our son was strong enough to roll away the great rock from the top of the hill, she would send him back to me.

"In the meantime I decided to mend my ways, and started my travels. The beautiful land I now rule over was in the hands of a monster king, who killed many of his subjects each year for his own pleasure. I fought and killed him and rescued his people. Then I married one of his daughters. I can't say I've been unhappy, but I've often longed for my first wife and my first-born son."

"My mother," said Thiga, half-sobbing. "When I left, she said I'd never see her again."

"That's true, my son," said the king. "She died the day you reached this land."

The queen and her sons were always jealous of Thiga, so although the king wanted to leave the whole of his kingdom to his eldest son, he was a wise man and divided his land equally amongst them all.

Not many years afterwards, the king lay dying. He called his sons to his bedside and asked them to keep peace amongst their people. Their father was an old man and because he was greatly respected, the sons all decided to agree to his dying wish. They each accepted their share of their father's kingdom, and all ruled wisely and well.

www.ingramcontent.com/pod-product-compliance
Lightning Source LLC
LaVergne TN
LVHW020419070526
838199LV00055B/3669